First American Edition 2009
by Kane Miller, A Division of EDC Publishing

First published by Esslinger Verlag J.F. Schreiber GmbH, Esslingen, Germany
Copyright ©2007 Esslinger Verlag J.F. Schreiber

For information contact:
Kane Miller, A Division of EDC Publishing
P.O. Box 470663
Tulsa, OK 74147-0663
www.kanemiller.com
www.edcpub.com
www.usbornebooksandmore.com

Library of Congress Control Number: 2009922111

Manufactured by Regent Publishing Services, Hong Kong
Printed December 2015 in ShenZhen, Guangdong, China

5 6 7 8 9 10

ISBN: 978-1-61067-435-5

Waiting *for* Winter

Sebastian Meschenmoser

Kane Miller
A DIVISION OF EDC PUBLISHING

"Winter is almost here," said Deer.
"I think it's going to snow."
"Snow?" asked Squirrel.
"Snow," answered Deer. "White
and wet and cold and soft."

Squirrel hasn't seen it snow.
He usually stays inside in winter.

But not this year!
This year, Squirrel is going to see it snow.

Any minute now …

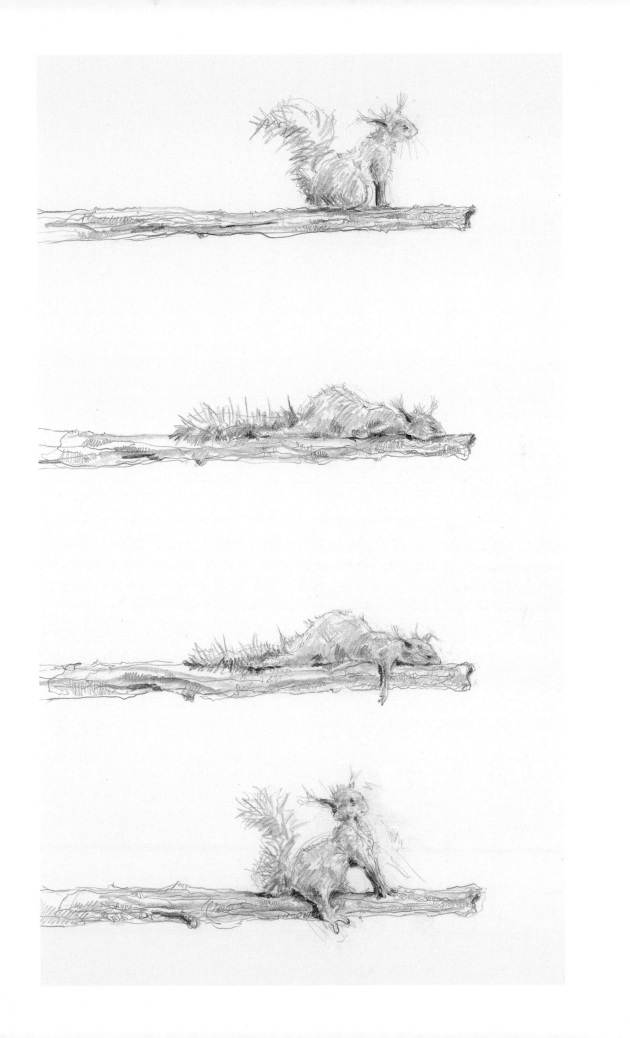

Waiting for snow is boring.

But what if Squirrel falls asleep?
He might miss it.

Exercise, thinks Squirrel.
Fresh air and exercise!

What is that noise?
Oh.
It's Squirrel.

Hedgehog hasn't seen it snow either, but now that he's awake he'd like to.

You'll have to **stay** awake, Hedgehog!

Uh-oh. Wake up!

Hedgehog doesn't think exercise and fresh air will work for him.

Squirrel has an idea.

"What about singing?"

Sea shanties!

Bear has had it.

No winter?
No snow?

Then no peace for Bear.

Bear will have to help
Squirrel and Hedgehog
watch for snow.

"White and wet and cold and soft,"
That's what Deer said.

But what if the first snowflake has already
fallen?
What if it is lying around somewhere?
What if it's already winter?

Hedgehog found it!
White and wet and cold,
it's the very first **snowflake!**

Winter will be wonderful
when it snows properly.

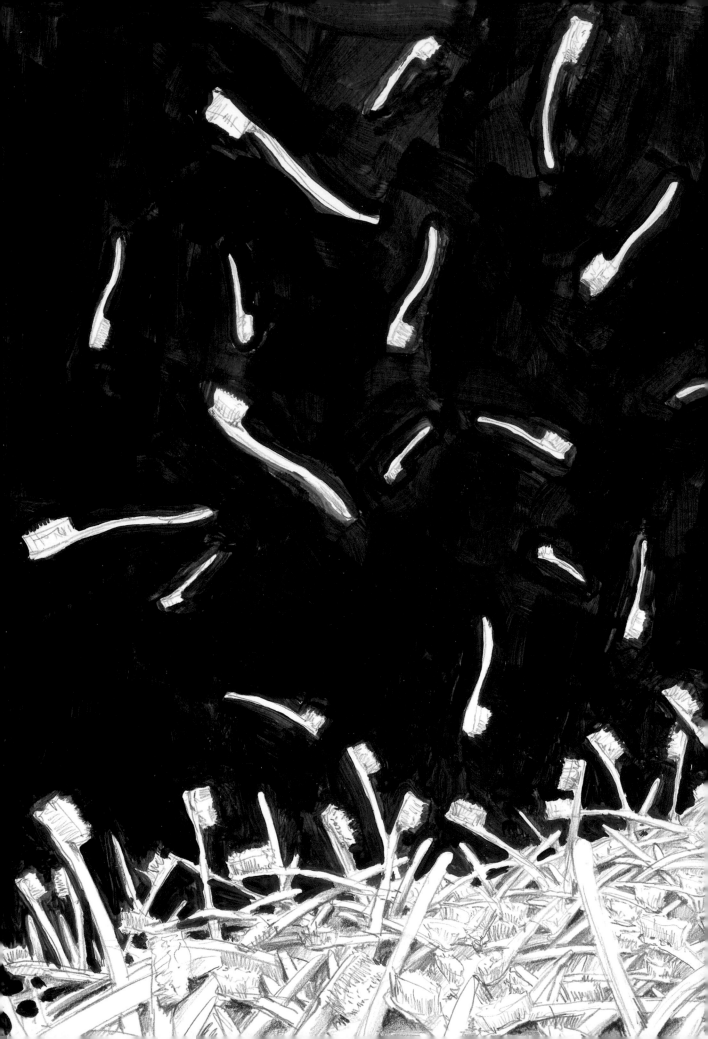

The first snowflake! Squirrel has it!

It's white and cold, and inside, it's a little wet.
Winter will be wonderful!

Bear is speechless.
Because what they have found is,

white and **wet** and **cold**,
but not soft at all!

It's a good thing that **he** has found it.

The very first snowflake!

Winter will be wonderful!

(But the snow is a little smelly.)